THE LITTLE HOUSE

THE LITTLE HOUSE

AN ARCHITECTURAL SEDUCTION

Jean-François de Bastide

Translation and introduction by Rodolphe el-Khoury
Preface by Anthony Vidler

PRINCETON ARCHITECTURAL PRESS

PUBLISHED BY
PRINCETON ARCHITECTURAL PRESS
37 EAST 7TH STREET NEW YORK, NY 10003
ISBN 1-56898-017-5

ORIGINALLY PUBLISHED IN FRENCH AS
La petite maison (1879)
LIBRAIRIE DES BIBLIOPHILES, PARIS
ENGLISH TRANSLATION ©1996 RODOLPHE EL-KHOURY
ALL RIGHTS RESERVED

99 98 97 96   4 3 2 1
FIRST EDITION
PRINTED AND BOUND IN THE UNITED STATES

BOOK DESIGN AND EDITING
Allison Saltzman

LIBRARY OF CONGRESS CATALOGING-IN-PUBLICATION DATA
Bastide, Jean-François de, 1724–1798
[Petite Maison. English]
The little house: an architectural seduction/Jean-François de Bastide; preface by
Anthony Vidler; introduction and translation by Rodolphe el-Khoury.
p. cm.
ISBN 1-56898-017-5
1. Small houses—France—History—18th century—Fiction.
2. Interior decoration—France—History—18th century—Fiction.
3. Aesthetics, French—18th century—Fiction.
I. Title.
PQ1955.B715P4813 1995
843'.5—dc20   95-21834
CIP

COVER IMAGE
François Boucher, Le Magnifique (1747), engraving by De Larmessin (detail).

For a free catalog of other books published by Princeton Architectural Press,
call toll free (800) 722-6657
Visit Princeton Architectural Press on the web at http://www.designsys.com/pap

CONTENTS

ACKNOWLEDGEMENTS

I would like to thank Anthony Vidler for introducing me to *La Petite Maison*; his initial investment in the text is at the origin of this translation. Credit and much gratitude is due to Nadia Benabid and Arthur Denner for their assistance in the translation and to Fares el-Dahdah and Christina Woods for their revision of the first draft. My thanks as well to Robert Darnton, Joanna Dougherty, Monique Mosser, Paulette Singley, and Georges Teyssot for excellent suggestions. From Princeton Architectural Press, I thank Kevin Lippert for his unwavering confidence in the project and Allison Saltzman for her skills in editing and graphic design. The greatest debt is to the Princeton University School of Architecture and Ralph Lerner, the Dean, whose generous contributions—intellectual and financial—have made this project possible.—*R. eK.*

The text of Jean-François de Bastide's *La Petite Maison*, as Rodolphe el-Khoury notes in his introduction to this translation, is given its peculiar force by the "marriage" of two literary genres: the erotic libertine novella and the architectural treatise. Indeed, it was very probably the result of a first collaboration between the writer Bastide and the architectural educator Jacques-François Blondel, a collaboration that lasted until Blondel's death and the publication in 1774 by Bastide of Blondel's equally remarkable *L'Homme du monde éclairé par les arts*, a work that might be considered among the first attempts at modern architectural criticism, itself a mixed genre somewhere between literature and architectural theory. In both these examples, one genre serves to offer an alibi for the other. Where Bastide in 1774 provided a writer's cover for Blondel to step beyond the bounds of professional etiquette and criticize his own students and contemporaries in print, so for the novelist, architecture and its meticulous description was a device for holding eroticism within the bounds of propriety, or *convenance*, constructing a wall, so to speak, between the pleasantly erotic and the simply pornographic. Both texts, further, were cast in the larger fiction of the didactic narrative—the sensory education of Mélite and the exemplary instruction of architectural amateurs and clients—in an age where education was purportedly an aim beyond reproach. Eroticism often adopted this ruse, from the anonymous *L'École des filles* (1655) to Laclos's *Les Liaisons Dangereuses* (1782) and de Sade's *La Philosophie dans le boudoir* (1795).

The attachment of eroticism to sites, spaces, and ultimately to gardens and architecture, however, formed part of a longer tradition of writing and ritual, one first sketched in the allegorical divagations of the classics, and practiced in the temples of Priapic cults, but that was given its modern literary form in the Renaissance, with the publication of the erotic-architectural epic, the *Hypnerotomachia Poliphili* in 1499. Here, with the aid of detailed illustrations, the reader was invited to learn the secrets of ancient architecture through the pleasant conceit of a love poem. This strange text, whose dream-like form and architectural specificity has led to speculation that its anonymous author was not Francesco Colonna but Leon Battista Alberti himself, also, importantly enough for its future influence, took on the guise of a utopian narrative along the lines of Filarete's didactic town designed for his patron Ludovico Sforza. In its utopian dimensions, the erotic community is depicted as at home, not only in buildings and their extensions, but in entire sites and landscapes, creating a protected world within the world.

In the task of establishing a world apart, the role of *space* is crucial. In the first place, space operates to set boundaries, establish limits, and resist encroachment; in the more fundamental sense of the erotic narrative, space suspends the supreme moment for an infinity, defending the all-too transitory act of love from time, day-to-day routine, and, of course, the inevitable process of aging. Space offers a place in which to escape from history. Such a role for space, implicit in the very form of "no-place," was to be explicitly noted in an erotic story written by a younger contemporary of Bastide, the archeologist and writer Dominique Vivant de Non, whose *Point de Lendemain (No Tomorrow)* published in 1777, carried the message in its title. Indeed, in this short tale, the place of eroticism in architecture and architecture in eroticism is suddenly reversed, as when, intrigued by the description of his lover's secret room, the narrator bluntly avows: "I was very curious: it was no longer Madame de T*** that I desired, but her *cabinet*," thus reinstating architecture as the primary object of eroticism.

It was also in the 1770s that the more directly architectural consequences of this marriage began to be evident in the work of one of Blondel's students, Claude-Nicolas Ledoux, first in his designs for *petites maisons* for the courtesan Madame Du Barry and the dancer Mademoiselle Guimard (designs at once criticized and praised in Blondel's *L'Homme du monde*), and then in the elaboration of projects for a new, ideal town, associated with the building of a saltworks near the forest of Chaux in Franche-Comté. This saltworks town, appropriately enough sited in a river valley popularly known as the Val d'Amour, was to become the object of Ledoux's obsession until his death, and the publication of his ideal projects and utopian text in another didactic treatise, *Architecture considerée sous le rapport de l'art, des mœurs et de la législation* (1804), a work which, according to a close friend of the architect, was based on his enthusiastic reading of the *Hypnerotomachia Poliphili*. Ledoux's utopia contained designs for many *petites maisons*, most notably one that he dubbed an *Oikéma*, the Greek word for "small house," commonly understood to signify a brothel or *maison close*. The function of the *Oikéma* was, with appropriate Enlightenment instrumentalism, more explicit than Bastide's little house. In its institutional form it was modeled on a number of projects for officially administered brothels in Paris, proposed as hygienic measures by writers such as Rétif de la Bretonne; in Ledoux's text, it took on the air of an orientalist conceit. In its architectural form, however, it took the notions of "character" and "propriety" (*caractère* and *convenance*) seen by el-Khoury as the operative figures of the erotic ambience, to an extreme. Preserving the proprieties in its external guise as a Greek temple, only in its plan did its role of moral purifier through sexual initiation become clear. Its passage-like arcade of bedrooms and alcoves ranged along a two-story gallery leading to an oval garden salon, all surrounded by pools, dining rooms, and dance halls, were combined in an unmistakably phallic plan, recalling the priapic temples engraved by Piranesi on the Campio Marzo, and studied by erotic *érudits* like Richard Payne Knight.

Ledoux's little architectural joke, where only the architect himself was privy to the plan and its signification, was perhaps, like Bastide's novella, among the last erotic narratives to preserve the classical *convenances*. Certainly when the Marquis de Sade described the mise-en-scène for the rituals of the *Cent-vingt jours de Sodome* (1785) or when Charles Fourier imagined his new communities of *amour social*, the fiction of "architecture" as traditionally understood, was dropped in favor of an art of endless mechanical manipulation of space— a kind of literal parallel to the mechanization of eroticism in their texts through repetition and systematization. Throughout the nineteenth century, and until the invention of psychoanalysis, eroticism was to be obsessed by the material devices of vision, elaborating a kind of voyeuristic mechanics with the aid of shutters, peep-holes, projectors, and eventually, cameras. There was likewise to be little room for the secret and arousing chambers of desire in the cool and transparent environments of modernism—if there is a place for the erotic in

Le Corbusier's urban utopias, it would be in the suspended fear of the void of infinite space, *l'espace indicible*, and in the pleasure of the superman who overcomes this fear. Banished to the furtive encounter in the marginal spaces of latrine and underpass, modern architectural eroticism, as Jean Genet understood, was less a question of *convenance* than of its complete demise.

It is in this context that Georges Bataille's redefinition of the word "espace" in his idiosyncratic lexicon of *Documents*, takes on special significance. True, his first qualification of the word is as *Question des convenances*. But the *convenances* of which he speaks are very different from those of the classical canon, or rather, even as they rely on former canons, establish entirely new mixed genres of space and eroticism. Bataille's examples, reinforced by carefully chosen photographs, refer not to the erotic charge of spaces of taste, nor to the functionalized spaces of erotic practice, but to the more fundamental eroticism of spatial transformation in itself.

For Bataille, "space can become one fish who eats another," or, equally, "a monkey dressed as a woman should be only one of the divisions of space." Traditionally conventional space, such as that of a prison, is indeed only perceptible in its full force when caught in the act of passing from one space to another, as in the moment of collapse; Bataille, didactic to the last, speculates that "evidently, no one has thought of throwing the professors into prison *to teach them what space is* (for example, the day when the walls collapse in front of the bars of their cell)." This imagined collapse of the Sadian universe, which was, after all, anticipated by de Sade himself, was, for Bataille, an opening onto a world of unmitigated eroticism in unimaginable freedom from the *convenances*. Despite its evident differences to the transparent world of Le Corbusier, such a realm of infinite slippage, of absolute cruelty and sacrifice, demands an equally Nietzschean soul for its appreciation. What perhaps Le Corbusier and Bataille failed to register, in their excited anticipation of modern post-eroticism, was the extent to which every-day eroticism, the undisputed province of the bourgeois reader, has, and always will, require its proprieties and its professors, its regulations and its boundaries, for best effect; the extent, that is, to which sexuality and space will always be an architectural affair.

I. ARCHITECTURE IN THE BEDROOM

The exterior, the visible, the surface of the objects
indicate their interior, their properties; every
external sign is an expression of internal qualities.

Lavater, *La Physignomie*

Jean-François Bastide's *La Petite Maison* belongs to an eighteenth-century literary genre combining fictional narrative with didactic observations on art and architecture.[1] Michel de Frémin's *Mémoires critiques* (1702) had explored the formula in an epistolary format and *L'homme du monde éclairé par les arts* (1774), co-authored by Bastide and Jacques-François Blondel, followed along the same lines.[2] The hybrid genre is often construed as a pedagogical device aimed at potential patrons who possessed material wealth and social status but lacked the necessary instruction for the appreciation of finer architecture. *La Petite Maison*, an intersection of the libertine novel and critical commentary on architecture, could certainly claim a wider readership among a lay audience.[3] But beyond marketing strategy and pedagogical aim, the mixture of genres fulfills literary and philosophical ambitions: the conjunction of aesthetics and eroticism sets up a narrative and theoretical framework for demonstrating much-debated theses on sensation, affect, and desire.[4]

The term "petite maison" refers to a specific building type that dates from the beginning of the Régence: garden pavilions or suburban retreats—in the Faubourgs Saint-Honoré and Saint-Martin, in Auteuil, Passy, Vaugirard, Neuilly, Clichy, and Bercy—which remained a staple fixture in eighteenth-century libertine fiction long after they were built and used as secluded quarters for clandestine encounters.[5] Few of these buildings have survived in the encroaching city, but many literary references along with hundreds of police reports suffice to evoke their memory and convey the importance they once assumed in the staging of libertinage.[6] During the Régence, these elegant retreats were known as "folies," in reference to the shield of foliage erected against the voyeurism of passers-by. The adoption, by the mid-eighteenth century, of the term "petite maison," was due not to the size of these *residences secondaires* (they were not necessarily small), but to a chain of semantic slippages in popular Parisian humor: the term "folie" literally means madness, and the Hôpital des Petites Maisons was the *résidence de choix* for lunatics.[7]

"I know personally nothing more decent than a *petite maison*," writes Claude Crébillon *fils*, "I am even inclined to think that their necessity has made them fashionable." The *petite maison* hence reconciles convenience with *bienséance* in a discrete refuge for scandalous liaisons: "what could be more pure, more sustained and discreet than the pleasures savored there!"[8] The factor of secrecy does not outlive the Régence, as the increasing notoriety of the *petite maison* lends a greater visibility to this coveted affectation of libertinage: "The *petites maisons* are no longer an asylum of mystery. Everyone knows who has stayed there, it is no secret who their owners are, and soon they will be putting their names on plaques outside the gates."[9]

Bastide's novella narrates a plot of seduction that gradually unfolds in the course of a visit to a *petite maison*. Architecture is a central element of the narrative. As a subject of lengthy and precise descriptions, it literally mobilizes the greater part of the text: the visit proceeds with careful attention to the building's architectural conception and its integration of painting, sculpture, and furniture in decoration. Furthermore, the text is annotated with detailed references to all the artists, cabinet makers, gardeners, and craftsmen involved with the project. As a site, pretext, and instrument for seduction, the architectural motif also guides the narrative at a constitutive level: the *petite maison* provides a basis for the formulation of the plot (the wager); it is also the agent of its development and resolution (the visit). As a spatial and temporal model for the narrative, the architecture of the *petite maison* is built into the very structure of the text: the episodic format of the narrative mirrors the parti of the *petite maison*, and the whole work is thus shaped according to its symmetry and *ordonnance*.[10]

The protagonists enter the house from the court (*côté cours*) and visit the right wing in the first half of the narrative. The temporal dimension of the narrative is calibrated to the spatial hierarchy of the apartments and is translated into dialogue and description of corresponding lengths. The action then moves outside into the garden for the turning point of the plot—the first embrace—and inside again, through the central door of the mirrored *salon* on the garden (*côté jardin*), with the second half of the narrative proceeding in a different tone, through the left wing of the house.[11]

The parti of the house conforms to established rules of *bienséance* in a hierarchical disposition of public and private spaces. But unlike the rectilinear suites of the traditional *hôtels particuliers* and *maisons de plaisance*, this compact plan maximizes communication across tightly clustered rooms. A likely academic model for this *petite maison* is Jacques-François Blondel's project for a house "*à l'italienne.*"[12]

A more direct and concrete source is unmistakable in the *petite maison* of the Fermier-Général Gaillard de la Boissière (also Bouëxière or Boixière). Considered one of the masterpieces of French architecture among Bastide's contemporaries, the so-called Pavillon de la Boissière (1751) was set in an elaborate and generously proportioned garden, designed by Jean-Michel Chevotet, on the Rue de Clichy. Primarily due to its architectural virtues, this *petite maison* attracted a lot of attention among architects and libertines alike; the King himself was known to have been one of its many admirers and faithful visitors. La Boissière was designed by Mathieu le Carpentier; his influence on *La Petite Maison* is obliquely acknowledged in the text: "Even le Carpentier himself could not have arranged anything more agreeable or more perfect."[13]

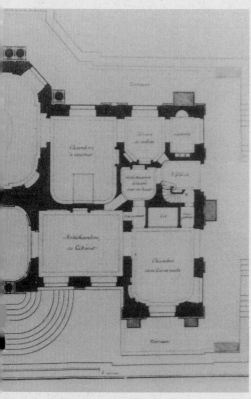

ne (1737–38), plan of main floor.

Elévation du côté de l'Entrée

Jacques-François Blondel, Maiso

à l'Italienne (1737–38), front elevation.

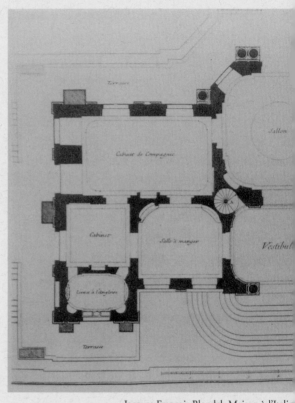

Jacques-François Blondel, Maison à l'Italie

Coupe et profil sur la longueur

...nne (1737–38), side elevation and transverse section.

Jacques-François Blondel, Maison à l'Italie

ne (1737–38), garden elevation.

Élévation de la façade latérale

Jacques-François Blondel, Maison à l'Ital

On a more theoretical level, Bastide's architectural vision is largely informed by the writings and teachings of Jacques-François Blondel, who had institutionalized *convenance* and heralded *distribution* as a new art, "the art of planning each suite of rooms to meet the often conflicting requirements of display and comfort."[14] *La Petite Maison* accordingly reconciles the proper needs of contemporary life with the elegance and luxury required for an "asylum of love" by ingeniously disposing a set of individually shaped, highly ornate, and programmatically specific spaces in a formal sequence of convenient adjacencies. Thus the water closet is accessible both from the bathroom and the living spaces, it is equipped with a modern valved basin, and it could rival the more public rooms in the exquisite taste of its decoration and furnishings. Furthermore, the water closet is adjacent to a wardrobe that conveniently connects with the vestibule, "where a concealed stair led down to a mysterious mezzanine."[15]

Distribution and *convenance* in *La Petite Maison* are further articulated in the adaptation of the decoration to the particular "function" of the room.[16] In comparison to the right wing of the house, the apartments on the left are "altogether of a different taste," while within each wing, adjacent rooms compose a sequence of contrasting tones and shifting moods. The fine-tuning of a nuanced taste to the *distribution* thus extends the nascent theory of character into the interior realm.[17] *La Petite Maison* deploys a sequence of scenes where painting, sculpture, and ornament are staged in sensational tableaux of different tastes. The theatrical inspiration is clear and is also evident in the dramatic use of lighting and in the machinery of spectacle and illusion;[18] the *table machinée*, or flying table, in the dining room and the illusory grove in the boudoir are notable examples.[19]

Another analog for the scenographic itinerary can be found in the picturesque garden, becoming fashionable in France at that time. Shortly following the publication of *La Petite Maison*, the picturesque was explored in a multitude of new treatises and translations: the literature of the new aesthetic articulated what Bastide had merely evoked in the traditional language of *goût* and *sentiment*.[20] Assimilating the lesson of the picturesque garden, an architecture of successive decor with varied characters is theorized and systematically prescribed in Nicolas Le Camus de Mézières's *Le Génie de l'architecture ou le rapport de cet art avec nos sensations* (1780):

> Each room must have its own particular character. The analogy, the relation of proportions, determines our sensations; each room makes us desire the next; and this agitation engages the mind, holding it in suspense, in a kind of satisfying bliss.[21]

In *Le Génie de l'architecture*, and implicitly in *La Petite Maison*, the radical influence of an empiricist epistemology translates into a theory of architecture based on sensation and affect.[22] The emphasis is on the mode of reception: proportion, order, symmetry. In short, the rules of architectural composition are reframed from the angle of a perceiving subject.[23] Dimensions, shapes, colors, and materials are determined and composed according to desired effects and anticipated reactions. The task of the architect is to design sensation: to orchestrate objects of character with subjective tastes.

Le Camus de Mézières favors a "theory of associations" that assigns fixed sensations and corresponding affects to specific types or characteristic forms: "each object has its own character; a simple contour is enough to express it."[24] The dynamic of taste in Bastide's text is more faithful to the "original" Locke and his French followers: qualities are not inherent to the object; they are projections or constructs of an active psychology. Taste takes an active role in production of sensation: not only does it comprehend characters or discern flavors, it can also project a willful desire.[25] In Bastide's theater of sensation, the stage comes alive only in the spotlight of a voracious desire and omnivorous taste.

Taste should give a soul to all the productions of art.
Jacques-François Blondel, *Cours*

La Petite Maison describes an intimate relationship between a host, a guest, and a building. Trémicour, the host, is "a man of wit and taste...magnificent and generous." Mélite, the guest, "had never played the coquette, and had yet to take a lover; time that other women squandered in love and deception, [she] spent in instruction, acquiring true taste and knowledge." He challenges her to visit his *petite maison* after she had frustrated his usually irresistible advances. "So they called it a wager and there she went." The building itself is an active participant in this unlikely ménage à trois: not only is it "the setting and the instrument for an elaborate seduction,"[26] the catalyst that would provide the optimal ambiance and the necessary lubricant for the machinations of seduction, it furthermore engages the protagonists as the subject of a sublimated sexual drive. So when initially, the penetration of the house is skillfully delayed, the restless attitude of the host displays the excited impatience of sexual foreplay. And once the host and the guest step inside, the guest's sexual appetite is progressively aroused by the scenography of tasteful decor. She savors their distinct "tastes" with increasing pleasure and abandon, propelling the plot with her incremental loss of inhibition and the expression of repressed desire.[27]

As a tale of love awakened by architecture, *La Petite Maison* will seem implausible or even frivolous to a present-day reader, yet another literary trifle in the vast repertoire of Baroque marginalia. If *La Petite Maison* is now seriously considered by some scholars, it is solely for its documentary account of decorative practices in the mid-eighteenth century. In recent critical commentary on the text there is indeed hardly any mention of the psychological process that propels the visit and the corollary plot of seduction. The emphasis is invariantly on the objects, even though the subjects of the architectural experience have the same level of articulation in the text.

More than a playful pretext for a catalog of decorative motives, the psychological framework elaborated by Bastide is precisely adjusted to the architectural structure of the narrative. The text is very thorough in describing decorative details; it is no less systematic in accounting for their effects on the receiving subject. But unlike the objective elements whose documentary insights are readily accessible, the subjective contents have become more opaque with historical distance. Commenting on such instances of opacity in eighteenth-century literature, Robert Darnton argues that "the perception of that distance may serve as the starting point of an investigation, for anthropologists have found that the best point of entry in an attempt to penetrate an alien culture can be that where it seems to be most opaque."[28]

The notion that architecture could inspire lustful designs is totally foreign today; the tendency is to trivialize it as a fanciful narrative twist that was concocted for the amusement of eighteenth-century readers, to dismiss it as a literary device that has little pertinence in historical analysis. The anecdotal or rhetorical inflation is unmistakable in Mélite's infatuation with architecture; yet hyperbole is most effective when grounded—however tenuously—in reality. An investigation of the text in relation to eighteenth-century culture might reveal the extent to which this "meaningful fabrication" is a reflection of actual aesthetic attitudes, beliefs, and modes of reception.[29]

The key to this investigation is the notion of taste, considered in its inherent ambiguities and historical vicissitudes. As a pivotal element in Bastide's text, it reconciles the quality of the object with the mode of its reception: decoration in good taste is savored by people of good taste.[30] It is instrumental to the intimacy which takes hold between the three protagonists (Trémicour, Mélite, and the *petite maison* itself), primarily in its tendency to oscillate between incarnate sensory perception and disembodied intellectual discernment; the capacity, in short, to blur the distinction between the beautiful, the desirable, and the edible.

The first discussion at the *Académie Royale de l'Architecture* was launched in 1672 with the question: "What is good taste?" For the next century, architectural theorists sought practical and theoretical answers to this problem. The romantic movement eventually relegated the issue to the periphery, while it instead focused on invention and expression in the act of artistic creativity. The preoccupation with taste coincided initially with the pursuit of equilibrium and *justesse* in a culture of *honnêteté* and *bienséance*, and was bound to become incompatible with the "great passions" of the romantic vision. In the eighteenth century, however, the emancipation of taste from a doctrinal classicism and its reorientation toward an aesthetic of subjectivity allowed for Dionysian modes of engagement with beauty and the sublime, and encouraged the meeting of the aesthetic and the erotic.

Architectural criticism in the seventeenth century tended to confine the sphere of taste to an aesthetic of "rules" based on the objectivity of a potentially quantifiable and analyzable language. As a faculty of critical discernment, taste tended to merge with judgment and came to designate the apprehension of rules as much as their application.[31] In the eighteenth century, the mechanisms of taste were recast in psychological terms. Under the dominant influence of an English empiricist epistemology, the sensuous categories of knowledge were rehabilitated: the apprehension of art became strictly aesthetic—i.e., sensuous—and its psychological mode was grounded in the "natural harmony" of the world. The aesthetic writings of the Abbé Du Bos, the Père André, Batteux, and Diderot, together with commentaries on the subject by Voltaire, Montesquieu, and Briseux, reorganized the origin, mechanism, and finality of taste in relation to Nature, sensation, and pleasure.

Taste was identified with a natural faculty and, more or less literally, with a sensory organ for the apprehension of the beautiful, *le sens interne du beau*: "It is this sixth sense within us, whose organs we cannot see."[32] The purpose of aesthetic apprehension was also linked to taste, "which is nothing other than to discover quickly and keenly the degree of pleasure that each thing should afford us," and was realigned with pleasure.[33]

In *Le Traité du Beau essentiel* (1742) Briseux accordingly theorizes the analogy of human and natural organizations to account for the psychological mechanisms of aesthetic pleasure:

> Since this universal mother [Nature] acts always with a single wisdom and in a uniform manner, we could rightfully conclude that the pleasures of seeing and hearing consist in the perception of harmonic relations as analogous to our constitution. This principle applies not only to music but to all the arts since the same cause could not have two different effects.[34]

The pleasure derived from the experience of the beautiful is thus due to a sympathetic rapport with the subject of beauty; the intensity of the pleasure is furthermore calibrated to the resonance or *intimacy* of this sympathetic rapport:

> If proportions in music have a greater impression on the soul than do those in other objects

of sensation, it is because music is more in sympathy with it, being more alive, so to speak. So pronounced is this sympathy that we are more touched by a human voice than by the sound of instruments.[35]

When the subject of beauty comes to life in the intimacy of aesthetic rapport, the theory of taste coincides with the theory of love.[36] The equation is most often noted in the case of gustative sensation. Gastronomy and eroticism have overlapped since the tasting of the forbidden fruit, but the oral proclivities of Eros were particularly pronounced in the eighteenth century, when the libertine was typically known to match sexual excess with gastronomical indulgence.

Despite its undeniable occularcentrism, the aesthetic discourse of the enlightenment repeatedly appealed to the mouth in order to demonstrate the immediacy and perspicacity of aesthetic apprehension: "We taste the stew, and even without knowing the rules governing its composition, we can tell whether it is good. The same holds true for painting and other products of the intellect that are intended to please us by *touching* us."[37] Half a century later, Voltaire's article "Goût" in the *Encyclopédie* still hinged on a rhetorical comparison of "the ability to distinguish the tastes of our foods" and "a feeling for beauties and defects in all the arts."[38]

Such comparisons were commonplace and consistently converged on the tactility of taste.[39] The gustative analog stressed the immediacy of apprehension in taste, the direct sensory contact with matter.[40] It projected a virtual tactility onto a visual mode of apprehension, which operated at a distance from the object of its assimilating faculty. This distance—spatial and conceptual—is momentarily abolished in the virtual tactility of a latent or *ideological* carnality. Thus implying haptic sensation in optic discernment, taste could *naturalize* and describe its aesthetic assimilation in a kind of tactile vision, combing the immediacy of touch with the distance of sight.[41] The tactile vision of taste could also be deployed as an organ of desire in the amorous rapport with architecture.[42]

1   Jean-François de Bastide, "La Petite Maison," *Le Nouveau spectateur* no. 2 (1758): 361–412. Republished in *Contes* vol. II (Paris: 1763), 47–88. This translation is based on the nineteenth-century edition, *La Petite Maison* (Paris: 1879). Bastide (1724–1798), a prolific writer who had gained some notoriety in the eighteenth century (Madame de Pompadour was one of his readers), was mostly appreciated for novels and plays dealing with *l'amour galant*: *La Trentaine de cythère*, *Le Tribunal de l'amour ou les causes célèbres de cythère*, *Les Ressources de l'amour*, *Les Graduations de l'amour*, etc. He would have been lost to oblivion had *La Petite Maison* not been exhumed by the Bibliophile Jacob and republished in the collection *Les chefs-d'oeuvres inconnus* in 1879.

2   Frémin's *Mémoires critiques* (Paris: 1702) contrives an architectural treatise into a series of letters sent by a man who dabbles in architecture to a friend who plans to build a house. The epistolary format is meant to provide a pleasurable reading experience accessible to those outside the field of architecture. Blondel and Bastide's *L'Homme du monde éclairé par les arts* (Amsterdam: 1774) also adopts the format of the epistolary novel to address a lay audience. It chronicles the romantic intrigues of a connoisseur of architecture and the arts with two

women, one of whom is sensual and instinctive, the other cool and intellectual—an ideal combination of characters for a great variety of amorous and aesthetic relations. Reports describing the tempestuous triangular affair are punctuated by dissertations on sculpture, painting, and architecture in "a most bizzare assemblage [un assemblage des plus bizarre]," as one of the reviewers put it, who maintains that "one could not naturally comment to a lover on public buildings [il n'était pas naturel de faire dire à un amant des observations sur les édifices publics]." (*Année Litéraire* no. 5 [1774]: 187–188; quoted in Richard Cleary, "Romancing the Tome; or An Academician's Pursuit of a Popular Audience in 18th-Century France," *Journal of the Society of Architectural Historians* XLVIII [June 1989]: 149.)

3   The vogue for the libertine novel had started under the Régence. With Claude Crébillon's *L'Ecumoire* (Paris: 1734) and *Le Sopha* (Paris: 1742), its popularity reached unprecedented heights. Contributions to the genre ranged from Denis Diderot's tastefully erotic and philosophical *Les Bijoux indiscrets* (Paris: 1747) to the plainly pornographic *Le Portier de Chartreux* (Paris: 1741).

4   Notable in the historical lineage of this conjecture is Francesco Colonna's *Hypnerotomachia Poliphili* (1499), a love story in the guise of an architectural treatise, in which buildings substitute for the body of the protagonist's lover.

5   In Choderlos De Laclos, *Les Liaisons Dangereuses* (Paris: 1782), the Marquise de Merteuil, for example, seduces the Chevalier Danceny in a "Temple de l'amour," a "petite maison." See Todd A. Marder, "Context for Claude-Nicolas Ledoux's Oikema," *Arts Magazine* LIV (1979): 174–176.

6   Three other literary works whose narratives are entirely set in
a *petite maison* are noteworthy, but unlike Bastide's they are little
concerned with the physical qualities of the decor: *La Petite
Maison* (Paris: 1749), a comedy in three acts by the Président
Hénault; *Oeuvres de la Marquise de Palmarèze. L'Esprit des moeurs
au* XVIIIe *siècle ou la Petite Maison*...(Paris: date unknown), an
erotic pornographic proverb by Ménard de Saint-Just, destined
for salacious entertainment in private theaters; *Le Souper* (Paris:
1771), an anonymous novel that met with considerable success
and seems to have been inspired by Bastide in the sparse descrip-
tive passages: "Here all the furniture flaunted voluptuousness;
once you step inside these enchanted quarters, you feel that you
are in the temple of pleasure, you are consumed with a desire for
sacrifice even if you had to serve as the victim."

7   See Michel Gallet, *Stately Mansions: Eighteenth-Century
Paris Architecture* (New York: 1972).

8   Claude Crébillon Fils, *Les Egarements du coeur et de l'esprit*
(Paris: 1745), quoted in Guy Richard, *Histoire de l'amour en
France* (Paris: 1985), 198.

9   Charles Pinot Duclos, Les Confessions du comte de M...,
(Paris: 1942), quoted in Richard, *Histoire de l'amour en France*,
op. cit., 199. Increasingly notorious *petites maisons* inspired a
proposal that a tax be levied on such *residences secondaires*.
Police records also show that they were an object of suspicion
and surveillance. Yet other sources suggest that the *petites
maisons'* aura of scandal had more to do with myth than reality.

10   The original version of *La Petite Maison* devoted lengthier
passages to the psychology of the characters and was abridged

in the 1763 edition. The architectural descriptions, however, remained intact.

11 The visit to the house proceeds like an initiation, promising the revelation of some knowledge after a series of ordeals. The structure of the initiation organizes many such narratives where architecture and love share center stage. A notable example is Vivant Denon's *Point de lendemain* (Paris: 1777). Monique Mosser underscores the paradigmatic role of the eighteenth-century garden in the spatialization of initiation rituals:

> ...every initiation entailed ritual journeys—that is, a succession of specific moves corresponding to the "ordeals" which symbolize the essential moral and spiritual evolution of the future initiate. Now the space of the garden lends itself ideally to this sort of symbolic circuit, to almost ritual perambulations in which the *fabriques* became compulsory stages.

Monique Mosser and Georges Teyssot, *Histoire des Jardins* (Paris: 1990), 274.
Another formal model may also be found in the rituals and spatial organization of Masonic lodges. See Anthony Vidler, "The Architecture of the Lodges," in *The Writing of the Walls* (Princeton: 1987).

12 The design was published initially in *De la distribution des maisons de plaisance et de la décoration des édifices en générale* (Paris: 1737), and was reprinted repeatedly in Blondel's subsequent works.

13 Other possible sources include le Carpentier's Hôtel Bouret (Rue Grange-Batelière, 1752), Etienne-Louis Boullée's

early hôtels, and Jacques-Ange Gabriel's pavilion for Madame de Pompadour at Choisy. The precedents are multiple and the influence of the novel no less important. Upon closer scrutiny, *La Petite Maison* proves to be an echo chamber for a thriving architectural sensibility and not a mere fancy of libertine literature.

14   Anthony Vidler, *Claude-Nicolas Ledoux: Architecture and Social Reform at the End of the Ancien Régime* (Cambridge, MA: 1990), 50. Beginning with Perrault's elaboration of beauty on the positive foundation of "reasonable convenance and the aptitude of every part to its intended use [la convenance raisonnable & l'aptitude que chaque partie a pour l'usage auquel elle est destinée]," the notion of *convenance* emerges as an important principle in classical theories of representation. In the latter part of the seventeenth century, and throughout the eighteenth, it refers to the fine calibration of rhetorical means and devices to the social status of patrons. *Convenance* thus regulates the relationship of an institutional hierarchy of architectural embellishments with social codes and conventions. By the mid-eighteenth century, *convenance* also suggests an intrinsic agreement between purpose, situation, and form. In Blondel's *Architecture Française, convenance* ceases to solely mediate decorative and social codes; it becomes an essential principle governing the production of architecture. In *La Petite Maison, convenance* legislates relationships internal to architecture and reconciles *distribution* with decoration according to *destination*: "For the sense of *convenance* to reign in a plan, it is imperative that each piece be situated according to use and with respect to the nature of the edifice. Its form and proportions should be relative to its purpose. [Pour que l'esprit de convenance règne dans un plan, il faut que chaque pièce soit située

selon son usage et suivant la nature de l'édifice, et qu'elle ait une forme et une proportion relatives à sa destination.]" Jacques-François Blondel, *Architecture Française* (Paris: 1752), t. 1, 26.

15   Such concealed spaces were a common feature of the sexual imaginary in the eighteenth century. In Andréa de Nerciat's *Felicia ou mes fredaines*, an extended labyrinth of libertine pleasures was accessible through a counterweight elevator that moved in a padded shaft between the two floors of a seemingly ordinary house. Sir Sydney, the operator of the premises and a consummate voyeur, could monitor the entire labyrinth from a secret room between the two floors that was connected to each bedroom by acoustic tubes and peepholes in the columns.

16   To speak of "function" would be anachronistic in this context. The proper term, *destination*, could also be translated as "purpose."

17   Between the publication of *L'Architecture Française* (1752) and the *Cours d'Architecture* (1771–77), Blondel is increasingly preoccupied with the character of different building genres and the impression they leave on the spectator. The *Cours* offers a vast repertoire of building types—sixty-four in total—each identified by the appropriate character, or more precisely, by the "natural" character of the "species." Character, in the *Cours*, is shown to depend upon the conception of the building as a whole—in the disposition of masses—more than in the symbolic power of decoration. Hence its initial relegation to the exterior and its delayed extension into interior *distributions*. By the late eighteenth century, the acceptance of character as an essential aspect of architecture is almost unanimous; in 1788, the theory is thoroughly formalized in the longest article—thirty pages—of Quatremère de Quincy's *Dictionnaire Methodique*.

18   Another model for the machinery of spectacle, however distant, is Nero's Domus Aurea. It was well known among erudite antiquarians and archaeologists and stood as a paradigm for antique luxury and ingenuity. Suetonius's often quoted description is most evocative:

> ...elsewhere all was overlaid with gold, and bright with jewels and mother-of-pearl. There were dining-halls whose coffered ivory ceilings were set with pipes to sprinkle the guests with flowers and perfume. The main dining-hall was circular and it revolved constantly day and night, like the universe...

Suetonius (Nero, 31-1, 2).

19   The grove scene certainly boasts the most memorable decor. The grove was built in a slightly different version by Etienne-Louis Boullée as a salon for the Hôtel d'Evreux, and no doubt inspired Claude-Nicolas Ledoux's winter garden in Madame Guimard's hôtel. The description of the illusory grove, the most often quoted passage in this text, was also appropriated in Nicolas Le Camus de Mézières's prescriptive account of the ideal boudoir. The taste for decorative illusion and trompe-l'oeil was not only characteristic of the Rococo period; it was perfected during the reign of Louis XVI, when "drawing rooms simulated the interiors of summer houses, and dining rooms presented the appearance of arbors. Putti carried off bedroom curtains into the heavens." Gallet, *Stately Mansions*, op. cit., 134.

20   Notable among such publications are: Claude-Henri Watelet, *Essai sur les jardins* (Paris: 1770); Nicolas Duchesne, *Traité de la formation des jardins* (Paris: 1775); Jean-Marie

Morel, *Théorie des jardins* (Paris: 1776). Most influential was François de Paul Latapie's translation of Thomas Whateley's *Observations on Modern Gardening* (London: 1771).

21   Nicolas Le Camus de Mézières, *Le Génie de l'architecture ou le rapport de cet art avec nos sensations* (Paris: 1780), 45.

22   British empiricism had an important influence on the Philosophes. Etienne Bonnot Condillac's *Essai sur l'origine des connaissances* (Paris: 1746), one of the most influential works of the eighteenth century, was specifically conceived as a response and critique to John Locke's *Essay Concerning Human Understanding* (London: 1689). The empiricist tendency of the French Enlightenment was in general inflected by Locke's epistemology.

23   The shift in favor of reception is stated in the introduction, proposing a regrounding of the orders on psychological bases:

> Architects have heretofore worked with the proportions of the five orders....But so many artists have only used the orders mechanically, without ever grasping the advantages of combining them into a whole with a distinctive character, capable of producing particular sensations. They have not comprehended more felicitously the analogy and the relation of these proportions with the affects of the soul. [Jusqu'ici on a travaillé d'après les proportions des cinq ordres d'architecture....Mais combien d'artistes n'ont employé ces ordres que machinalement, sans saisir les avantages d'une combinaison qui put faire un tout caractérisé, capable de produire certaines sensations; ils n'ont pas conçu plus heureusement l'analogie & le rapport de ces proportions avec les affections de l'âme.]

Le Camus de Mézières, *Le Génie*, op. cit., 1–2.

24   Ibid., 3.

25   The role of desire in determining will and sensation was argued by Condillac in the *Traité des sensations* (Paris: 1754).

26   Vidler, *Claude-Nicolas Ledoux*, op. cit., 51.

27   The precise categories of a psychoanalytic interpretation are beyond the scope of this analysis. The processes of the Freudian unconscious are evoked loosely, in a generic use of "sublimation" and "repression." But my interpretation of Bastide's novella remains *literal*—literal in the sense that it does not unravel or exhume a hidden meaning. In *La Petite Maison*, the economy of desire is laid bare in the process of the narrative itself, in the structure of the plot, the initial contract, the visit, the procession, and the ultimate transference. The meaning of *La Petite Maison*, in short, *is already psychoanalytic*.

28   Robert Darnton, *The Great Cat Massacre and Other Episodes in French Cultural History* (New York: 1984), 78.

29   The term "meaningful fabrication" is borrowed from Robert Darnton's cultural history or "ethnological *explication de texte*." It is meant to emphasize the historical significance of fiction in the construction of "reality":

> Like all story telling, it sets the action in a frame of reference; it assumes a certain repertory of associations and responses on the part of the audience, and it provides meaningful shape to the raw stuff of experience. But since

we are attempting to get at its meaning in the first place, we should not be put off by its fabricated character. On the contrary, by treating the narrative as fiction or *meaningful fabrication*, we can use it to develop an ethnological *explication de texte*.

Darnton, *The Great Cat Massacre*, op. cit., 78.
Bastide's fabrication is explicitly fictional; its literary effect and historical-cultural significance do not depend on the potential credibility of the narrated events. The role played by the taste of architecture in awakening erotic desire might indeed have stretched the limits of eighteenth-century verisimilitude; it is yet demonstrative or symptomatic of a particular mentality.

30   Bastide's use of the term "goût" often overlaps with "caractère"—a term shared with natural scientists such as Linnaeus, Buffon, and Adanson, whose taxonomical procedures relied upon the identification of "general and particular characters." The terms *goût*, *génie*, and *caractère* do tend to overlap and are often interchangeable in eighteenth-century texts. At the risk of oversimplification, one might distinguish their distinct semantic spheres by situating them along the different stages of the cycle of production and consumption. Taste is accordingly a fundamental precondition of genius; character is the imprint or mark left by genius in the work; taste, again, is the receptive faculty that can discern character. Thus taste encapsulates the system, as it is a condition of both production and reception.

31   See Françoise Fichet, *La Théorie architecturale à l'age classique* (Brussells: 1979), 36.

32   Jean-Batiste Du Bos, *Réfléxions critiques sur la peinture et sur la poësie* vol. II (Paris: 1719), 342; (repr. Geneva: 1967), 225.

33   Montesquieu, "Goût," in Denis Diderot and Jean le Rond d'Alembert, *Encyclopédie ou dictionnaire raisonné des sciences, des arts et des métiers, par une société des gens de lettres* (Neuchâtel: 1751–1777), 762.

34   Charles-Etienne Briseux, *Traité du Beau essentiel* (Paris: 1742), 45.

35   Ibid., 47.

36   One could also speak of the taste of love. Hence the following definition in the apocryphal letter of Ninon de Lenclos:

> L'amour, pris comme passion, n'est qu'un instinct aveugle,
> ...un appétit qui nous détermine pour un objet plutôt que
> pour un autre sans qu'on puisse donner la raison de son goût.

Nino de Lenclos, *Dialogues* (Paris: 1750), 117, quoted in René de Planhol, *Les Utopistes de l'amour* (Paris: 1921), 124.
This definition does however suggest a point of divergence between taste and love: love is characterized by a capricious will whereas taste has a persistent intersubjective normativity. One could predict the (desirable) object of taste but not that of love. This divergence dictates a strategy for seduction in *La Petite Maison*: the predictably tasteful architecture of the house should awaken and captivate the subject's love so as to guide or channel it to the object that it had capriciously rejected.

37   Du Bos, *Réfléxions critiques* , op. cit., 341/225 (emphasis added).

38   Voltaire writes that aesthetic taste

is like that of the tongue and the palate: a ready and unre-
flective discernment, sensitive and sensual in appreciating
the good, violent in rejecting the bad, often lost and uncer-
tain, not even knowing if it should be pleased by what is
presented to it, and sometimes forming only by dint of
habit. [Est un discernement prompt comme celui de la
langue & du palais, & qui prévient comme lui la réflexion;
il est comme lui sensible et voluptueux à l'égard du bon; il
rejette comme lui le mauvais avec soulèvement; il est sou-
vent comme lui, incertain & égaré, ignorant même si ce
qu'on lui présente doit lui plaire, & ayant quelquefois
besoin comme lui d'habitude pour se former.]

Voltaire, "Goût," in Diderot and d'Alembert, *Encyclopédie*, op.
cit., 761.

39   Etymologically, the tactility of "taste" is more evident than
"goût." It is related to the French "tâter," and its definition
includes "touch, grope, feel, explore by touch, to have carnal
knowledge of..." as immediate antecedents to "perceive by the
sense of taste." (*Oxford English Dictionary*)

40   "Taste is not content with seeing, with knowing the beauty
of a work; it has to feel it, to be touched by it. [Il ne suffit pas
pour le goût de voir, de connaître la beauté d'un ouvrage; il
faut la sentir, en être touché.]" Voltaire, "Goût," in Diderot
and d'Alembert, *Encyclopédie*, op. cit., 761.

41   The relationship between sight and touch was an obsession
in the eighteenth century. Most notable is the debate generated

by the Molyneux (1656–1698) problem. Initially reported in Locke's *Essay Concerning Human Understanding*, op. cit., the problem is later addressed in the writings of Diderot, Condillac, and Jean-Jacques Rousseau. In the *Lettres sur les aveugles*, Diderot paraphrases it as follows:

> Suppose one blind from birth has been taught to distinguish by touch a cube and a sphere of the same metal and approximately the same size, so that when he touches them he can say which is a cube and which is a sphere. Suppose the cube and the sphere placed on a table and the blind man suddenly to see; can he distinguish the cube from the sphere by sight without touch?

Margaret Jourdain, ed. and trans., *Diderot's Early Philosophical Works* (Chicago: 1911), 118–119.

42   Nonvisual modes of assimilation and other senses are of course involved in the experience of the *petite maison*. They conform to the logic of the spectacle and do not challenge the supremacy of sight—the privileged perceptual apparatus in the projection of desire. In *La Petite Maison*, the scents of violet, jasmine, and rose are wonderously perceived—they are released from the varnish of woodwork—and music is magically heard at a sign from the host—it is performed by musicians hidden behind a partition. In both cases, the cause or source of sensation is inaccessible and incomprehensible to the *spectator*. The senses are disoriented and the feeling is one of wonder and bewilderment: the pleasures of scents and music are diffused and intoxicating, they belong to the global *éblouissement* of the spectacle.

THE LITTLE HOUSE

Mélite took to the company of men with great ease, and only kindly souls and the best of friends did not consider her a flirt. Her uninhibited manner, her airy talk, and a certain abandon were ample proof. The Marquis de Trémicour had his mind set on her seduction, and felt assured of an easy success. With more reason than most men, he could expect to profit from feminine impulsiveness. A man of wit and taste, he was maginficent and generous, unrivaled in his charm. Yet despite these many assets, Mélite resisted him. He could not imagine anything so odd. She told him she was virtuous; he would never believe her to be so.

It was constant war between them on this subject. At last, the Marquis challenged Mélite to come to his little house, a *petite maison*. She answered that she would come, and that she would not fear him there, nor anywhere else. So they called it a wager and there she went, knowing not what a *petite maison* was, only the name. She did not realize that no other place in Paris or all of Europe was as charming and as artfully contrived for love. Let us follow her there, then we shall soon see how she fared with the Marquis.

Trémicour's remarkable house stood on the banks of the Seine. An avenue extending from a *patte d'oie* led up to the gate of a lovely grass-covered forecourt, on either side of which were symmetrically arranged yards. One contained a menagerie of wild and domesticated animals, as well as a charming dairy, decorated in marble and shells, and kept cool by abundant and pure waters that tempered the heat of the day. Here one also found all the necessities for the maintenance of the carriages, and a storehouse for the numerous and varied provisions a delicate and sensual life requires. In the other yard was a double stable, a riding ring, and a kennel of dogs of every breed.

All these structures stood behind a simply decorated facade of a rustic and pastoral character that owed more to nature than to art. Ingeniously arranged openings in this wall allowed glimpses of endlessly varied orchards and vegetable gardens, and all these things were so remarkable in their attractions that hardly had one's gaze alighted on one than it was drawn impatiently to the next.

Though attracted by the sights beyond the wall, Mélite wanted first to explore the beauties closer to hand. Trémicour, however, was anxious to lead her inside, where he could divulge his love for her.

Already, Mélite's somewhat excessive curiosity had begun to annoy the Marquis. He responded distractedly to her compliments on his good taste, and for the first time, the house meant less to him than the object he had brought to it. Mélite noticed his impatience, and triumphed in it. Curiosity alone would have compelled her to linger at every turn; mischief incited her even more. Thus doubly motivated, she had all the more reason to be stubborn: a question here, a compliment there, exclamations everywhere!

"Truly," she chirped, "this could not be more ingenious!"

"How charming!" she murmured, "I have never seen such..."

"But the apartments are much more remarkable," he replied, "you shall see. Won't you come inside?"

"In a while," she persisted, "this is just as important; we must see it all. Now, there is something here we have not yet seen. Please, Trémicour, no need for impatience."

"I have none, Madame," he responded, slightly vexed. "I merely speak in your own interest. I fear that you will tire yourself with all this walking, and will not be able to..."

"Oh! Forgive me," she interrupted, mockingly;

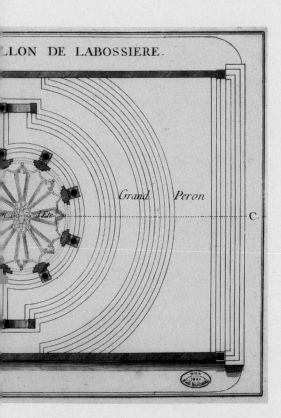

LLON DE LABOSSIERE.

Grand   Peron

Trapo... d'Eté

C.

ière (1751), plan of main floor.

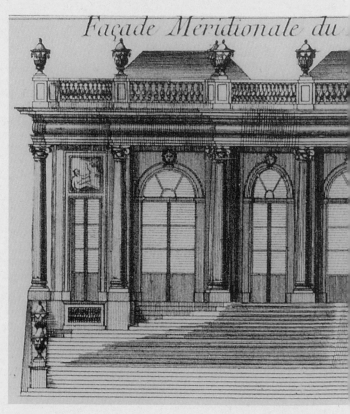

Façade Méridionale du

Mathieu le Carpentier, Pavillon

Pavillon de Laboueœiere.

Boissière (1751), front elevation.

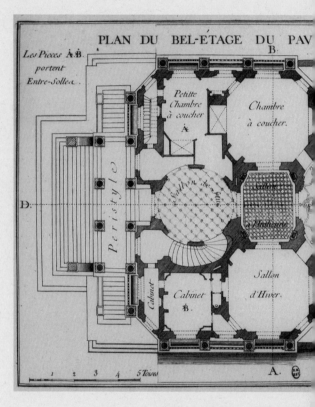

PLAN DU BEL-ÉTAGE DU PAV

Les Pieces A.B. portent Entre-Solles.

B.

Petite Chambre à coucher A.

Chambre à coucher.

Peristyle

Sallon de ..ille

...ullon à Plotheque

D.

Cabinet

Cabinet B.

Sallon d'Hiver.

1   2   3   4   5 Toises

A.

Mathieu le Carpentier, Pavillon de la B

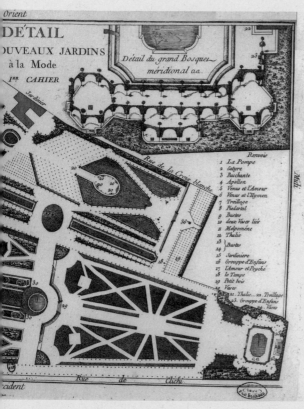

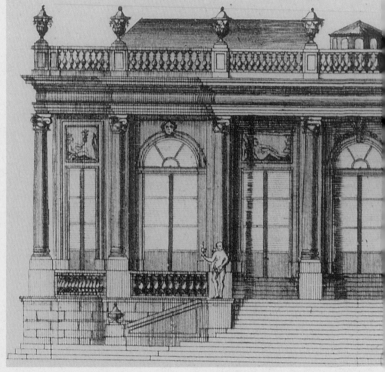

Façade Septe

Mathieu le Carpentier, Pavillon de la Boi

ère (1751), garden elevation.

PLAN GÉNÉRAL DES N[...]

DU JARDIN

de M. de Laboſſiere

ou de la Bouexiere

Orangerie

Septentrion

Pavillon

25 la Peinture
26 27 la Muſique
28 la Geographie
29 4. Vaſes du
Japon
30 Vaſe de Marbre
31 Apollon
32 Herodote
33 Venus
34 Satyre
35 Bacchante
+ Statues et Grouppes
de marbre
n Autres Statues
36 Andromede

Entrée

A Paris chez le Rouge Ruë des Grands Auguſtins.

Jean-Michel Chevotet, Pavil[...]

"I did come here to walk, and I am feeling quite strong."

Trémicour endured Mélite's stubborn chattering for another quarter of an hour. If he had not finally detected her capriciousness, he might have abandoned the venture altogether, out of sheer exasperation. He took her hand and drew her closer and closer to the house; two or three times, she seemed to acquiesce, and would let herself be brought just so far, and then, after a few steps, would naughtily go back to examine once more what she had seen already. She was trying Trémicour's patience; he continued coaxing her along until it seemed as if he were walking on thorns.

Mélite laughed to herself and gave him enticingly demure looks that seemed to beseech his kindness, but instead, declared unabashedly and unmistakably: "Your despair is my delight." Finally, Trémicour let fly a cutting remark. Mélite pretended to find him unkind, and called him intolerable.

"It is you who is intolerable!" he cried. "You promised that you would see everything, yet we remain here. I like my apartments and I want you to see them."

"Very well, Marquis! Let us see them then; no need to quarrel. Good God, how impatient you are!" All this was spoken with a voice so gentle and eyes so sweet that he felt his shortcomings merely furthered.

"Indeed, I am impatient," he admitted. "But I hope you haven't forgotten the agreement that brings you here, Madame."

"Not in the least," she answered, walking on. "Quite the contrary, I'm playing my role far better than you. You told me your house would seduce me; I wagered it would not. If I now fall prey to its charms, am I unfaithful to our agreement?"

Trémicour was about to reply, but they had reached the center of the main courtyard, and Mélite's gasp at her first glimpse of it cut him short. Small but perfectly proportioned, the courtyard spoke well of the architect's taste. It was surrounded by a wall of fragrant trellises high enough to screen off the main building but not so high as to impede the course of the bracing breeze. Trémicour accepted Mélite's continuing flood of tiresome compliments, but his thoughts were elsewhere; they had arrived at a perron leading up into a rather large vestibule. At this point, Trémicour dismissed the valets, sending them off to their quarters with a wave of his hand.

He led Mélite directly to a salon that opened onto the garden, a salon unequalled in all the universe. He noticed Mélite's delight and permitted her to pause and contemplate its finery. Indeed, so voluptuous was this salon that it inspired the tenderest feelings, feelings that one believes one could have only for its owner. The salon was circular in shape, capped with a dome painted by Hallé.[†] The lilac-colored paneling framed beautifully crafted mirrors. In the overdoors, Hallé had also painted

† One of our French painters, who, along with Boucher, was preeminent in the representation of fables.

Decoration of a vestibule, illustrated in Jacques-Fra

Blondel's *De la distribution des maisons de plaisance*.

scenes of love. The tastefully positioned sculptures were further enhanced by the luster of gold, and the drapes had been chosen to compliment the lilac of the paneling. Even le Carpentier[†] himself could not have arranged anything more agreeable or more perfect.

The day was drawing to a close and the light waned; a valet came to light the thirty candles held by a chandelier and by girandoles of Sèvre porcelain artfully arranged in their brackets of gilded bronze. These thirty candles reflected in the mirrors, and this added brilliance made the salon seem larger and restated the object of Trémicour's impatient desires. Mélite admired the room's beauty in earnest, and lost all interest in doing mischief to Trémicour. She had never played the coquette, and had yet to take a lover; time that other women squandered in love and deception, Mélite spent in instruction, acquiring true taste

† One of the King's architects, who excelled in the decoration of interiors. The *petite maison* of M. de la Boissière and the house of M. Bouret attest to his taste and genius.

Study for a fireplace, displaying the characteristic stylistic
ambivalence of the mid-eighteenth century. The decoration
described by Bastide consistently vacillates between the aging
intricacy of the *Style Rocaille* and the more fashionable
simplicity of neoclassicism.

and knowledge. She learned to recognize the works of the best artists at a glance. She looked on their masterpieces with respect and awe, while their true value was lost to most other women, who were capable only of whimsical love for trifles and triviality.

And so Mélite praised the light chisel of the ingenious Pineau,[†] who had created the sculptures. She admired the talents of Dandrillon,[††] who had applied his skills to convey the most imperceptible refinement in the carvings of the woodwork. Forgetting the folly of fueling Trémicour's vanity, she lavished upon him the praise that his selection and taste demanded.

"Delightful, simply delightful!" cried Mélite. "This is how the advantages of fortune should be spent. This is so much more than just a little house; this is a temple of genius and taste..."

[†] A sculptor famed for his ornamental designs, whose work adorns most of our *hôtel* interiors.
[††] A painter who discovered the secret of odorless paneling paint and the art of gilding sculpture with no primer.

"This is how the asylum of Love should be," he replied tenderly. "Without knowing this god, I feel that in order to inspire him, it should seem as though he inspired me."

"I couldn't agree more," said Mélite, "but tell me, why is it that I have heard it said that so many of these *petites maisons*, betray such bad taste?"

"Because their owners desire without loving. Because," he added, "Love has not decreed that you would one day accompany them there."

Mélite listened and would have listened longer had Trémicour not pressed a kiss against her hand, alerting her to his intention to be rewarded for every opportunity he took for flattery. She rose and asked to see the other rooms. The Marquis, seeing how touched Mélite had been, simply by the beauty of the salon, had better yet to show her. He trusted that she would be touched even more by more touching objects and thus hastened her to her destiny.

Trémicour took her hand, and they entered into a bedroom on the right. In the square-shaped

room, a jonquil-colored bed of Peking fabric, bro-
caded with resplendent hues, lay nestled in a
niche, across from one of the windows that overlooked the garden. This room, with chamfered
corners graced by mirrors, was crowned by a vault-
ed ceiling. In the ceiling's center was a circular
painting that brought all of Pierre's[†] mastery to
the image of Hercules in the arms of Morpheus,
awakened by Love. The room's walls were painted
a soft yellow; the marqueterie parquet combined
amaranth and cedar woods and the marble was a
Turkish blue. Lovely bronzes and porcelains were
displayed in a studied and orderly manner on the
marble-topped consoles that sat before each of
the four mirrors. Elegant furniture of myriad
forms resonated the ideas expressed everywhere in
the little house, and coerced even the coldest
minds to sense something of the voluptuousness it
proclaimed.

[†]   One of our famous French painters, known for his mastery
of color.

Mélite no longer dared praise anything; she had begun to fear her own emotions. Thus, she hardly spoke. Trémicour could have taken offense, but he was studying her, and he was a keen observer; her distress did not escape his notice. He would have even thanked her for what he knew was appreciative silence, were he not aware of the peril of premature gratitude, expressed while it is still within a woman's power to disclaim the thoughts for which she is being thanked.

Mélite entered the next room to find yet another hazard. This room was a boudoir, a place that needs no introduction to the woman who enters, her heart and soul recognizing it at once.

The walls of the boudoir were covered with mirrors whose joinery was concealed by carefully sculpted, leafy tree trunks. The trees, arranged to give the illusion of a quincunx, were heavy with flowers and laden with chandeliers. The light from their many candles receded into the opposite mirrors, which had been purposely veiled with hanging gauze. So magical was this optical effect that the boudoir could have been mistaken for a natural woods, lit with the help of art. In a niche was an *ottomane*, a sort of resting bed that lay on a parquet of checkered rose wood. It was hung with fringes of gold and green, and was strewn with pillows of various sizes. The walls and ceiling of the niche were also covered with mirrors; the woodwork and the sculpture were painted in hues appropriate to the scenes they depicted.

Here again, the color was applied by Dandrillon,[†] who had mixed his paints with the fragrances of violet, jasmine, and rose. All this decoration was also applied to a screen that concealed a spacious corridor, where the Marquis had arranged for musicians to play.

Mélite could scarcely contain her delight. She lingered in the boudoir for more than a quarter of an hour. Her tongue was mute, but her heart

† Again, we owe to this artist the invention that eliminated the foul odor of varnish. He also devised a method of mixing other scents in with the varnish. These scents linger on for many years.

Claude-Nicolas Ledoux, Pavillon Guimard (1770), section.
In the salon, also labeled winter garden on the plan,
trompe-l'oeil trees painted on mirrors evoke the illusory grove
in the boudoir of *La Petite Maison*.

could not be silenced: it cautioned her against men who orchestrate so many talents to express a sentiment that they are barely capable of themselves. Although Mélite made note of this suspicion, her mind stored it away at the bottom of her heart, where it would soon be lost. Trémicour sought out those thoughts with his piercing gaze, and destroyed them with his sighs. No longer was she sure that he was a man she could confidently reproach for the monstrous disparity between his desires and his deeds. He said nothing, yet his eyes spoke many promises. Still, Mélite doubted his sincerity; she was now able to see how well he could feign, and felt that such dangerous art in such a charming place exposed one to no end of treacherous temptations. To dispel this fearful thought, Mélite moved away from the Marquis toward one of the mirrors, pretending to readjust a pin in her coiffure. Trémicour stood in front of the opposite mirror, and with the help of this trick was able to watch her even more tenderly, without her having to look away. In seeking a moment's respite from Trémicour's charms, Mélite had fallen into an even deeper trap.

"Marquis," she snapped, realizing her mistake, "please stop looking at me! This is becoming quite tiresome."

He flew toward her.

"Do you truly loathe me?" he cried. "Ah, Mélite, a little less injustice to a man who needs not displease you to be convinced of his misfortune."

"How modest you are!" she mocked.

"Yes, modest and unfortunate," he continued. "What I feel tells me to fear, and what I fear tells me to fear even more. I adore you, yet I am at your mercy."

Mélite continued her jokes and pleasantries, but disguised her true feelings clumsily. Trémicour had taken her hand, and she had not thought to withdraw it. When he dared tighten his grip, she complained and asked if he wanted to cripple her.

"Ah, Madame!" he said, feigning despair. "I beg you to forgive me; I did not think one could injure so easily."

Trémicour's expression disarmed Mélite, and seeing that the moment was ripe, he gave a signal and the musicians hidden behind the screen began to play. Their concert disconcerted her; she listened only for a moment. Trying to flee a place that had become far too threatening, she entered, alone, into a new room, even more delicious than any she had yet seen. Trémicour could have taken advantage of her ecstasy to close the door without her noticing and force her to listen to his words of love, but he would rather that his victory progress at the pace of pleasure.

The room that Mélite had entered was a bathroom, in which nothing was spared: marble, porcelain, and mousseline were in lavish display. The paneling was adorned with arabesques executed by Perot[†] from designs by Gillot,[††] in frames of

---

[†]   A very skilled artist who, at Choisy, excelled with paintings in this genre.
[††]   The greatest of his time in the design of arabesques, flowers, fruits, and animals, Gilot surpassed even Perin and Audran in this field.

Design for a decorative panel in the arabesque genre
by Claude Gillot (c.1720).

impeccable taste. The walls were decorated with pagodas, crystals, and shells, along with bronzes by Cafieri[†] in seashore motifs, all combined with great discernment and skill. One of the bath's two niches was occupied by a tub, the other by a bed of embroidered Indian mousseline, hung with tassels.

Adjacent to the bath was a dressing room. The paneling, painted by Huet,[††] represented fruits, flowers, and foreign birds, interlaced with garlands and medallions in which Boucher[†††] had painted cameos of gallant subjects matching his designs on the overdoors. A *toilette* of silver crafted by Germain was also featured prominently.[††††]

[†] A great sculptor, Cafieri is known for the bronzes that adorn the interiors of all the beautiful houses in Paris and its environs.

[††] Another painter famous for his arabesques, and particularly for his depictions of animals.

[†††] The painter of the Graces, and one of the most ingenious artists of our century.

[††††] A famous goldsmith and son of the greatest artist that Europe has seen in this field.

Deep-blue and gold porcelain vases overflowed with flowers. Tastefully upholstered furniture of aventurine wood, crafted by Martin,[†] added another fine touch to a room that, no doubt, could charm the gods. The Marquis had lavished no less attention on the room's ceiling; a flat dome with a golden mosaic of flowers, painted by Bachelier,[††] rose up above a frieze of gilded sculpture and an elegant cornice.

Mélite could not withstand so many wonders; she felt weak, stifled even, and was forced to sit down.

"I can not take this any longer," she said. "This house is too beautiful. There is nothing comparable on earth..."

Mélite's tone of voice betrayed a secret distress; Trémicour felt that she was nearly his. With all

---

[†] Martin is a famous varnisher whose reputation is known to everyone.
[††] One of the most skilled painters of our time in this particular genre. He subsequently gave it up to become a rival of Desportes and d'Oudry, and perhaps even surpassed their excellence.

the more skill, he resolved to give up his feigned earnestness and indulged in trifling with a heart that could still harden.

"You did not believe it so earlier," he told her, "yet this is how one learns that nothing is certain. I knew that all of this would charm you, but women always want to doubt."

"I no longer doubt," she replied. "I confess that all of this is divine and thoroughly enchanting."

He moved closer to her, with no affectation.

"Admit," he challenged, "that my *petite maison* is worthy of its name. Although you have reproached me for not feeling love, you will at least concede that so many things here capable of inspiring it should honor my imagination. Furthermore, I am convinced that you still fail to comprehend how one can possess an insensitive heart and such tender ideas all at once. Isn't it true that you think so?"

"Possibly," she answered with a smile.

"Well!" he resumed, "I protest against your misjudgment. I say this without any self-interest, since I see now that even with a heart that is a hundred times more gentle than the one you believe indifferent, I still could not move you. It is, however, certain that I, more than anyone else, am capable of love and constancy.

"Our gossip, our acquaintances, our houses, and our lifestyle all give us an air of lightness and perfidy, and a reasonable woman judges on these external aspects. We contribute ourselves willingly to this reputation when we are inclined to take this air of inconstancy and coquetry because common prejudice assigns it to our condition.

"Believe me, we are not always taken by frivolity nor pleasure itself: there are objects made to arrest us and bring us back to the true, and when we happen to encounter them, we are more in love and more constant than others....But you are distracted—what are you dreaming of?"

"This music," she said. "I thought I had escaped it, yet from afar it is but more touching." (What a confession!)

"It is love in your pursuit," he replied, "but it does not know with whom it is dealing....Soon this music will be nothing but noise."

"That is quite certain," she answered, "even now it irritates me....Let us get out, I would like to see the gardens."

Trémicour obeyed again. His docility was no sacrifice; no confession, no favor to a lover could match the pleasure he took in her confusion.

In passing, Trémicour showed Mélite a room that adjoined both the bath and the living quarters. This room was a water closet, where a valved basin of marble and fragrant wood marqueterie sat in a niche designed to imitate an arbor. The image of the arbor also graced the other walls of the room; it gathered at the curve of the ceiling into a *berceau*, where a central opening allowed a glimpse of blue skies and birds in flight. Urns and porcelains filled with fragrances were placed artistically on stands. The cabinetry, all beautifully painted, contained crystals, vases, and all the intimate items necessary for the use of this room.

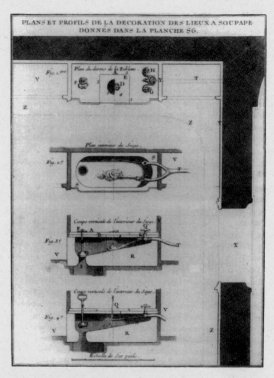

Illustration of a valved basin (flushing toilet) demonstrating
the new technology of comfort, in Jacques-François Blondel's
De la distribution des maisons de plaisance.

Mélite and Trémicour exited and went through a wardrobe where a concealed stair led down to a mysterious mezzanine. The wardrobe also opened onto the vestibule, which they crossed again on their way back to the salon. Trémicour opened the door to the garden, surprising Mélite with the breathtaking vista of an amphitheatrically arranged garden, lit by two thousand lanterns.

The foliage was still beautiful, resplendent in the studied lighting that reverberated in artfully disposed water jets and reflecting pools. Tremblin,[†] the lighting master, had gradually nuanced the lights by placing *terrines* in the proximity of the house, and lanterns of different sizes in the distance. At the ends of the main allées, he had set up illuminations of varied aspect to encourage closer scrutiny. Mélite was enchanted; for a quarter of an hour she uttered nothing but cries of admiration. The air was filled with fanfares

† One of the seasoned decorators at the Opéra and the *petits appartements* of Versailles.

played on rustic instruments, and farther away, a lone voice sung an aria from *Issé*.[1] Water gushed and splashed in charming grottos, and cascaded and flowed into rippling pools. In countless groves, countless games were offered for pleasure and for love. The gardens had been designed to imitate rooms; shrubs and trees created an amphitheater, a ballroom, and even a concert stage. Parterres of flowers, bowling greens, terraces, vases, and marble figures marked the limits and corners of all crossroads in the garden where dim lights created infinite variety and intrigue.

Trémicour wandered aimlessly, feigning nonchalance and even disinterest. Again, he was intent on concealing his ardor. He led Mélite into a narrow path, whose dimness did not fail to alarm her. They turned a sudden corner, to find nothing but more darkness. Usually a woman of confidence and poise, Mélite began to feel terribly ill at ease; everything had become dreadful, due to her secret unrest. At the height of her terror, a blast of artillery echoed through the gardens. Trémicour

Detail of the large trellis in the garden of
the Pavillon de la Boissiére.

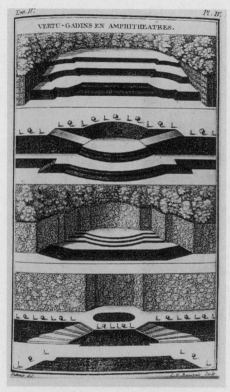

Garden terraces with an ampitheatrical layout, illustrated in
Jacques-François Blondel's *Cours*.

took advantage of Mélite's fright, and held her tightly. Affronted by this intimate gesture, she was about to free herself with equal vivacity when the sudden flash of fireworks revealed in the reckless man's eyes a deep and submissive love. She stood motionless for a moment, transfixed by his tender gaze. This moment was considerably longer than would have sufficed for her to tear herself from his arms, had she truly hated him. It was also long enough for Trémicour to glean that she had not merely hesitated, but had forgotten to pull away altogether. Of course, the fireworks display had been carefully planned beforehand; Trémicour had enlisted the skills of Carle Ruggieri.[†] The fireworks, of countless hues, burst open in the sky above a spray of water jets; it was an entrancing and delightful scene.

All this spectacle, all these wonders, further complimented a man who was far from lacking in

[†]   An ingenious Italian fireworks artist, often employed by the Court and the Princes.

charm. Mélite caught a glimpse of her fate in his amorous gaze, and in his expectant sighs, she heard the mighty voice of an oracle decreeing her defeat. She was seized with anxiety, and anxiety is stronger than nascent love: she sought escape.

"Well," she said, "this is all quite charming, but we must leave; I am expected elsewhere."

Trémicour understood that she should not be challenged, but he did not doubt his power to deceive her; he had succeeded a hundred times by yielding. He softly urged her to stay, but she did not want to. She began to walk faster, and her voice became agitated. Her words were incoherent or simply monosyllabic: though she fled she was still taken with object of her flight.

"I hope at least," he said to her, "that you will deign to take a look at the apartment to the left of the salon before you leave."

"It certainly could not be any more beautiful than anything I have seen already," she replied, "and I am in a hurry to leave."

"It is of a different taste altogether," he continued,

"and since it is unlikely that you will return here, I would be delighted..."

"No," she gasped, "spare me. Just tell me how it is, and that will suffice."

"I would agree, but we are already there, and it will take only an instant. Are you really in such a hurry? You did promise me to see everything, and unless I am mistaken, I believe you would regret not having legitimately won the wager."

"So it must be!" sighed Mélite. "You would otherwise boast for having lost in the first round only."

They were already back in the salon. Trémicour opened a door, and Mélite stepped, by herself, into a game room that overlooked the garden. She promptly proceeded toward a window that was flung open, glancing only hesitantly at the room. Maybe with some pleasure, she recognized in the view the place that she had just fled.

"You must admit," Trémicour said to her wickedly, "that this sight is delightful. Here is the place where we were just a moment ago."

Listening to his words, she further indulged the memory of the garden encounter.

"I do not understand," he pressed on, "why you did not enjoy the garden longer....All the other women who found themselves there seemed unable to leave."

"Perhaps they had different reasons for staying," suggested Mélite.

"So you have demonstrated," he sighed. "You could at least grace this room with your continued presence, which is more than you afforded the grove. Deign to consider it."

She thus abandoned the window, and examined the room in which she stood. The walls and furniture gleamed with fine Chinese lacquer, and the furniture was upholstered in embroidered fabric from India. Girandoles of rock crystal complemented exquisite porcelains from Saxony and Japan that were artfully placed on gilded stands.

Mélite admired several of the porcelain figurines. The Marquis beseeched her to keep them; she refused, but with such reluctant prudence that he was not denied the pleasure of the gesture. He thought it best not to insist and he recognized that though she might yearn, he ought not imply that she yearned quite so much.

The lacquered room had two or three doors. One opened into a comely little cabinet connecting with the boudoir; the other, into a dining room preceded by a pantry that was also accessible from the vestibule. The cabinet existed solely for the enjoyment of coffee. Just as lavishly decorated as the rest of the *appartements*, its walls were painted a watery green color, and were dotted with picturesque motifs enhanced with gold. A number of Italian baskets filled with flowers were placed about the room, and the furniture was upholstered in black moiré with an embroidered chain pattern.

Forgetting herself more and more, Mélite sat down, and began to ask one question after another. She went through all that she had seen, asking the prices of things and the names of artists and artisans. Trémicour responded to her inquiries and apparently had none to make himself. She praised him, commending his taste and brilliance, and he thanked her like a man to whom praise is rightfully given. His motives were so well disguised that Mélite, increasingly moved, considered everything that touched her only from the angle of genius and taste. She truly forgot where she was, that she was in a *petite maison*, in the company of a man who had wagered to seduce her with the beauties she now contemplated with so little inhibition and praised with so much candor. The sly Marquis seized this moment of pure delight to lead Mélite out of the room.

"Indeed, all this is very beautiful," he said, "yet I still have something more astonishing to show you."

"I find that difficult to believe," she said, "but considering all I have just witnessed, nothing now seems impossible and everything shall be seen." (This confidence comes naturally and will only surprise those who doubt anything because of ignorance or insensitivity.)

So Mélite stood up and followed Trémicour to

the dining room, where a table was laid out with an elaborate meal.[2]

"What is this?" she cried, stopping at the door. "I told you I had to leave!"

"Surely you cannot expect me to remember everything," he answered. "It is very late anyway; you must be tired, and since you have to dine sometime, you may as well do me the honor of granting me preference. By now you should know that very little risk is involved in this visit."

"But where are the servants?" asked Mélite. "Why this air of mystery?"

"They never come in here," he answered, "and I thought that it would be wise to dismiss them for the day. They gossip, and would give you a reputation—I respect you too much."

"Your respect is curious," she said. "It did not occur to me that I should have to avoid their gaze more than their imagination."

Trémicour feared he had not fooled her in this one ruse.

"You reason better than I do," he admitted.

"Now I see that simplicity would have been best. Unfortunately, they were indeed dismissed and there is nothing I can do to remedy that."

Although it was unclear whether Trémicour was again, being untruthful, Mélite thoughts were elsewhere; she did not bother to protest. She sat down distractedly, observing a revolving door in one corner of the room, through which they were served by unseen hands, at Trémicour's signal.

Mélite ate little and drank only water; she was distracted, distant, and wistful. The spell was broken; the spontaneous exclamations that had voiced her surfacing emotions were no longer heard. She was more preoccupied with her anguish than by the things that had caused it. Trémicour, animated by her silence, began telling her the wittiest tales (our wit with women often comes at the expense of theirs). Mélite smiled, but did not speak.

Suddenly, the table dropped down into the kitchen in the cellar, and from above, a new table descended to take its place. It promptly filled the gap left in the flooring, protected by a balustrade of gilded iron.[3] This feat, incredible to Mélite, roused her from self-absorption and invited her to consider anew the beauty and the ornamentation of the place that was offered for her admiration. For the first time, she noticed the walls, stuccoed by Clerici[†] in infinitely varied colors. The walls' panels were sculpted in bas-relief of the same material, created by the famous Falconet;[††] they depicted the feasts of Comus and Bacchus. Vassé[†††] had made the trophies that adorned the decorative pilasters, glorifying hunting and fishing, the pleasures of the table and the pleasures of love.[4] Mounted on each of the twelve trophies, candelabra with six-stemmed girandoles flooded the room with dazzling light.

[†]   A Milanese craftsman who gained a great reputation with his work in the Salon de Neuilly for the Conte d'Argenson, and more recently, the Salon Saint-Hubert, for his Majesty.
[††]   The King's sculptor, famed for his excellent works, many of which were exhibited at the salon.
[†††] Also the King's sculptor, who gained a reputation with his light chisel and his seductive Graces.

Designs for decorative trophies by Choffard (c.1750).

However struck by the room's splendor, Mélite glanced about tentatively, and returned her gaze to her plate. She had not looked at Trémicour twice, and had not uttered even twenty words. Trémicour, however, watched her closely and persistently; he found he could read her heart better than her eyes. The agitation in his voice betrayed the momentum of his delectable thoughts. Mélite listened, and the less she looked, the more she heard. His tormented voice made such an impression on her senses, soliciting her to look at the man who was expressing such love. For the first time, love was presented to her in its true character.

Mélite had been courted before, hundreds of times, but when a suitor is not particularly liked, his cares and attentions can hardly be mistaken for love. Nevertheless, such cares and attentions tend to disguise ulterior motives, and a reasonable woman learns to be wary of them early on. What seduced Mélite here was Trémicour's inaction in expressing such tenderness. Nothing alarmed her defenses, for she was not being attacked. She was being adored, and adored silently. She pondered all this; she returned his gaze. The candor in her eyes did not escape him; it encouraged him to ask her for a song. She had a charming voice, but she refused. He saw that the seduction was but momentary and protested with a sigh. He ended up singing himself; he wanted to prove to Mélite that he respected her resolve, and to demonstrate how love itself had given him the strength to comply with little constraint. He thus parodied Quinault's well-known lyrics from *Armide*:

Que j'etois intensé de croire
Qu'un vain laurier, donné par la victoire,
De tous les biens fût le plus précieux!
Tout l'éclat dont brille la gloire
Vaut-il un regard de vos yeux?

How mad I was to think
That bestowed by Victory, a vain laurel crown
Was the most precious of prizes!
All the radiance with which fame shines
Is it worth one look from your eyes?[5]

I did not follow the exact words he supplemented to Renaud's, still they ingeniously evoked the abjuration of inconstancy, including an oath to everlasting love. Mélite seemed touched, yet she smirked slightly.

"You doubt my words," he said, "indeed, I am in no position to be persuasive. I attracted you here with my frivolous wager; you came only to demonstrate a most justified disdain. Even solid proof would dissolve in the face of my reputation and I have only mere promises to begin with there! Meanwhile I most certainly adore you. Such is my misfortune, and it will never end."

Mélite did not want to answer; she felt that Trémicour was sincere and that she owed him something to repay his kindness. She thought that her indifference would make him miserable and so she looked at him with tenderness.

"I see that you do not want to believe me," he continued, "but at the same time I see that you cannot be entirely skeptical. Your eyes are more just than you are, they at least express pity..."

"How could I believe you, even if I wanted to? Do you forget where we are? Do you realize that this play house, this *petite maison*, has long been the theater of your deceitful passions, and that the same promises you make now have served the triumph of imposture a hundred times in the past?"

"Yes, I have thought about all this. I know that what I have said to you, I have said to others, and that it has always met with success. But while I used the same expressions, I was not speaking the same language. The language of love is in the tone. My tone never failed to betray my oaths. Today, it would hold up to them if you were just."

Mélite stood up (an unmistakable evidence of persuasion in someone who is not deceitful), and Trémicour ran toward her.

"Mélite, where are you going?" he pleaded, trembling. "If anything, you at least owe it to me to listen. Think how much I have respected you....Please be seated, you have nothing to fear: my love is your guarantee."

"I do not want to listen to you!" she cried, as she

began to withdraw. "What would my kindness lead to? You know that I do not want to love; I resisted everything. I would make you too unhappy..."

He did not stop her; he saw that in her confusion, Mélite had mistaken one door for another, and was about to enter a second boudoir. He let her go, but stepped on her dress when she was at the threshold, so that in turning her head to disengage her dress, she would not see the place she was entering.

This new room, next to which lay a wardrobe, was stretched with thick green gourgouran. The most beautiful engravings by Cochin,[†] Lebas,[††] and Cars[†††] were hung symmetrically on the walls. The room was lit just enough to allow the masterpieces of these skillful masters to be seen. The

[†] A very distinguished draftsman and engraver who succeeded, with much brilliance, the famed Callot, Labella, and Le Clerc.
[††] An engraver from the King's Cabinet, to whom we owe the beautifully printed collection of Tenieres's works.
[†††] Also an engraver, his prints perpetuated the talents of the masters with much artistry.

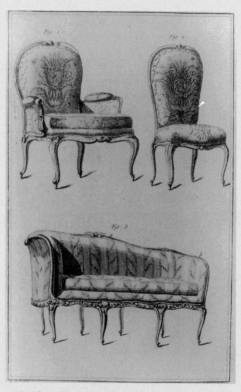

A plate from the *Encyclopédie* displaying different types of
upholstered chairs, including a bergère and an ottoman.

ottomans, the duchesses, the sultanes, were all lavished here.[6] Everything was charming indeed, but Mélite could stand it no longer. She recognized her error and wanted only to leave. Trémicour stood at the door and prevented her from passing.

"So, Marquis," she whispered in fear, "what is your aim, what do you mean to do?"

"To adore you and die of pain. My present state is unknown to me....I feel it taking hold of my entire being....Mélite, please listen to me..."

"No, I want to leave. I will listen when I am farther along, on my way out."

"I want you to love me," he continued, "I want you to know that my respect equals my love. You must not leave!"

Shaking with fear, Mélite felt faint; she collapsed almost into a bergère. Trémicour threw himself at her knees, and spoke to her with the eloquent simplicity of passion. He sighed, and even shed some tears. She listened, and sighed with him.

"Mélite, I will never deceive you; I know to respect a happiness that will teach me how to think, how to act. You will always recognize the same tenderness in me, the same ardor. Have pity on me! You see..."

"I see all too well," she said, "and this confession is quite telling. I am not foolish, and I am not false. What do you want from me? Trémicour, I am chaste, and you are inconstant..."

"Inconstant I have been indeed. But blame it on the women that I have loved, for they had no love to offer. But if Mélite loved me, if her heart could blaze for me, only the excesses of my unwavering zeal would remind her of my inconstant passions. Mélite, you see me, you hear me, and now you know my heart."

She was quiet, and he thought to take advantage of her silence. He dared...he was stopped, but with more love than he would have met in yielding.

"No!" said Mélite. "I am confused, but I still know what I am doing. You shall not triumph.

Let it suffice that I consider you worthy of it; prove your worth—I shall abhor you if you insist!"

"If I insist? Ah, Mélite..."

"Marquis! What are you doing?"

"What I am doing..."

"Trémicour, Leave me! I do not want..."

"Cruel woman! I shall die at your feet, or I shall obtain..."

The threat was terrible, the situation even more so. Mélite shuddered, faltered, sighed, and lost the wager.[7]

1   *Issé* is a *tragédie lyrique* by Houdard de la Motte set to music by André-Cardinal Destouches (1697). *Issé* was frequently performed at the Académie Royale de Musique, with productions featuring stage sets by Jean-Nicholas Sevandoni and François Boucher. The opera was a personal favorite of Madame de Pompadour, who arranged for its private presentation in the *petites appartements* of Versailles. She was thus represented in the guise of the heroine, in a celebrated painting by Boucher.

2   Such meals were called *repas en ambigu*. In fashion since the late seventeenth century, they consisted of a simultaneous presentation of more or less contrasting dishes in lieu of the usual consecutive courses. *L'Art de bien traiter* defines the *ambigu* as follows: "rather than splitting a meal into many courses, all the dished are presented together at the outset but in the right arrangement and with much order. The senses are thus so delighted that the most disgusted regain their appetite." The *ambigu* is distinguished primarily in its spatial organization. It does not necessarily rival a *souper* or a *collation* in the taste of individual dishes, but rather in the potential for elaborate formal compositions. The *ambigu* can be "so finely

laid out, that no picture, painting, spectacle, or decoration could rival it in richness and order." (L.S.R., *L'Art de bien traiter* [Paris: 1674], 359–360, 372–373.)

3   "Tables volantes" or "tables machinées" were built for royal residences such as Bellevue and Choisy, both by Guerin. One was also planned by Loriot for the *petit trianon* at Versailles, but was never built. Besides its spectacular virtues, this mechanical device was meant to provide total privacy to the diners by keeping the servants in the kitchen below. One of its multiple versions is described in the *Mercure de France*: "When the guests enter the room, not a single trace of the table would be visible; they see only a very even parquet with an ornamental rose at the center. At the slightest signal, the petals withdraw under the parquet and the served table springs up, accompanied by four dumbwaiters which rise through four openings at the same time." (Quoted in Claude Bonnet, *Écrits gastronomiques* [Paris: 1978], 64–65.)

4   On the same street as "La Boissière," the *petite maison* of the Duc-Maréchal de Richelieu—the notorious Don Juan of the eighteenth century—featured similar carvings in the panel-ing of the dining room. D'Argenson, who chronicled the reception given on 21 November 1740, relates this evocative anecdote: "A fine start to the supper was the sight of the old Duchesse de Brancas, eager to examine these figures, putting on her spectacles and, tight-lipped, coldly peering at them, while M. de Richelieu, candle in hand, explained them to her." (Quoted in Michel Gallet, *Stately Mansions: Eighteenth-Century Paris Architecture* [New York: 1972], 97.)

5   *Armide* is probably the most famous opera or *tragédie lyrique* composed by Jean-Baptiste Lully, with a Libretto by Philippe Quinault (1686). It remained a point of reference throughout the eighteenth century and was repeatedly the focus of the debates which opposed French and Italian music. The polemic precipitated the opera's demise, before it vanished completely with the Ancien Régime—until recent interest in French Baroque music revived it on the European stage. The story of Armida, which was initially told in Tasso's *Jerusalem Delivered*, is known in a variety of settings and was one of the most popular subjects at the opera, arguably because of the many opportunities it provided in showcasing the machinery of spectacle. Jean Starobinski has accordingly suggested that the seductive magic of the paradigmatic enchantresses— the Armidas, Medeas, Circes—can be identified with the essence of opera itself, with *opera as enchantment*. (Starobinski, "Opera and Enchantresses," in *Opera Through Other Eyes*, David J. Levin, ed. [Stanford: 1993].) In the structure, processes, and instruments of seduction, *Armide* bares evocative similarities and no less telling differences to *La Petite Maison*. The story goes as follows: about to kill Renaud, whom she had magically immobilized in a deep trance, Armide, the Saracen *magicienne*, has a weakness for the beauty of the heroic crusader. She decides to spare his life and keep him under the spell of her enchanting world. Renaud is eventually rescued from the seductive illusion, and Armide, who meanwhile had truly fallen in love with him, is left to suffer the price of her deception, alone in her magnificent palace.

6   Ottomans and sultanes are cushioned seats, day beds, or sofas without backs or arms. The duchesse is a kind of chaise-

longue, consisting of two armchairs facing each other that are joined by a stool or ottoman. Another version, usually called a duchesse brisée—broken duchess—is composed of a bergère and a foot stool. The bergère—literally, shepherdess—into which Mélite eventually collapses, is a large and easy armchair with a loose cushion or upholstered seat.

7 Bastide's original version of the story concluded with Mélite's retreat to the country after a difficult but successful resistance to Trémicour's advances in the green boudoir.

ILLUSTRATION SOURCES

COVER   Haldane MacFall, *Boucher* (London: 1908).

PP. 25–28 Jacques-François Blondel, *De la distribution des maisons de plaisance et de la décoration des édifices en général* (Paris: 1737–38).

PP. 61–64 Bibliothèque Nationale, Cabinet des Estampes, Topographie de Paris.

PP. 68–69 Jacques-François Blondel, *De la distribution des maisons de plaisance et de la décoration des édifices en général* (Paris: 1737–38).

P. 71   *Dessins originaux des maitres décorateurs* (Paris: 1914).

P. 77   Michel Gallet, *Claude-Nicolas Ledoux* (Paris: 1980).

P. 81   Thomas Arthur Strange, *An Historical Guide to French Interiors, Furniture, Decoration, Woodwork and Allied Arts* (New York: 1900).

P. 87   Jacques-François Blondel, *De la distribution des maisons de plaisance et de la décoration des édifices en général* (Paris: 1737–38).

P. 90   Bibliothèque Nationale, Cabinet des Estampes, Topographie de Paris.

P. 91   Jacques-François Blondel, *Cours d'architecture* (Paris: 1773).

P. 101   *Dessins originaux des maitres décorateurs* (Paris: 1914).

P. 107   Denis Diderot and Jean le Rond d'Alembert,
         *Encyclopédie ou dictionaire raisonné des sciences, des
         arts et des métiers, par une société des gens de lettres*
         (Neuchâtel: 1751–77).